LISA: BOOK TWO
THE TRAIL TO
GOLDEN
CARIBOO

PRISCILLA GALLOWAY

Lisa: Book Two

THE TRAIL TO GOLDEN CARIBOO

PRISCILLA GALLOWAY

PENGUIN
CANADA

PENGUIN CANADA

Published by the Penguin Group

Penguin Group (Canada), 10 Alcorn Avenue, Toronto, Ontario, Canada M4V 3B2
(a division of Pearson Penguin Canada Inc.)

Penguin Group (USA) Inc., 375 Hudson Street, New York, New York 10014, U.S.A.
Penguin Books Ltd, 80 Strand, London WC2R 0RL, England
Penguin Ireland, 25 St Stephen's Green, Dublin 2, Ireland (a division of Penguin Books Ltd)
Penguin Group (Australia), 250 Camberwell Road, Camberwell, Victoria 3124, Australia
(a division of Pearson Australia Group Pty Ltd)
Penguin Books India Pvt Ltd, 11 Community Centre, Panchsheel Park, New Delhi – 110 017, India
Penguin Group (NZ), cnr Airborne and Rosedale Roads, Albany, Auckland 1310, New Zealand
(a division of Pearson New Zealand Ltd)
Penguin Books (South Africa) (Pty) Ltd, 24 Sturdee Avenue, Rosebank, Johannesburg 2196,
South Africa

Penguin Books Ltd, Registered Offices: 80 Strand, London WC2R 0RL, England

First published 2005

1 2 3 4 5 6 7 8 9 10   (WEB)

Copyright © Priscilla Galloway, 2005
Cover and interior illustrations copyright © Sharon Matthews, 2005
Design: Matthews Communications Design Inc.
Map copyright © Sharon Matthews

Manufactured in Canada.

LIBRARY AND ARCHIVES CANADA CATALOGUING IN PUBLICATION

Galloway, Priscilla, 1930–
Lisa : the trail to golden Cariboo / Priscilla Galloway.

(Our Canadian girl)
"Lisa: Book Two".
ISBN 0-14-301679-2

1. Cariboo (B.C. : Regional district)—Gold discoveries—Juvenile fiction.
I. Title. II. Title: Trail to golden Cariboo. III. Series.

PS8563.A45L583   2005   jC813'.54   C2004-905413-9

Visit the Penguin Group (Canada) website at **www.penguin.ca**

To
my granddaughter Laney,
with love

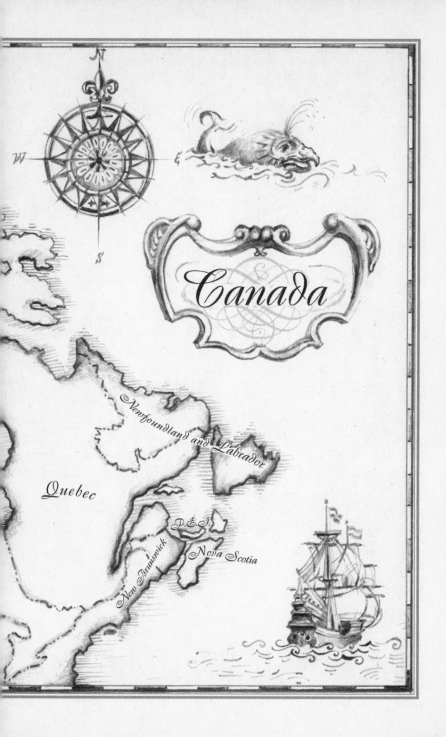

Canada

Newfoundland and Labrador

Quebec

P.E.I.

New Brunswick

Nova Scotia

ON THE TRAIL AGAIN

Bⁿⁿ RITISH COLUMBIA'S FUTURE was shaped by gold and Governor Douglas. When gold was discovered on the Fraser River (1858) and on Williams Creek in the Cariboo (1862), thousands of treasure-seekers flocked to the scene. In a gold rush, things happen quickly. Roads and bridges, wayside stopping places, and then towns sprang up. None of this building was easy, and all of it was expensive. However, British Columbia grew and developed early and quickly because of gold.

The major hero of this early development was Governor James Douglas. British Columbia was a colony of Britain, but many of the would-be miners came from California. Governor Douglas could see that if he did not act quickly in the name of Britain, the Americans would almost certainly take possession of the country, just because of their large numbers. He could not wait for months while letters went to London and orders came back to him.

Governor Douglas took action. He issued mining licences and required all would-be miners to purchase one. He appointed judges and established the rule of British law. Most importantly, he provided access to the mines by a wagon road through high mountains and across raging rivers. British Royal Engineers built the first part of it; they investigated and surveyed routes; they laid out townsites. Private contractors completed the road in 1865. The work was partly financed through the mining licence fees.

In Book One, *Overland to Cariboo,* in 1862, Lisa and her family left Fort Garry, now Winnipeg, and joined a group of almost two hundred men bound for the Cariboo. The epic five-month journey brought Lisa's family to Kamloops just as winter was closing in. Papa Schubert found work with the Hudson's Bay Company. Although he had left Fort Garry to go mining, the stories Papa Schubert heard that winter did not encourage him to uproot the family again.

Many gold-seekers tried to make a fortune in the Cariboo, but few succeeded, and almost nobody made a fortune and kept it. Men in rags, who had spent their last penny, struggled back down the trails. Even in

Kamloops, Papa Schubert heard plenty of tales of failure and misery.

We pick up Lisa's story in the early months of 1863. By spring, Lisa was very restless in Kamloops. She longed to reach the Cariboo and become a miner. So when an invitation arrived from Archibald McNaughton, a friend from the long trek overland, to travel with him and his new wife to the Cariboo and live with them as a companion and helper, Lisa leapt at the chance. Book Two, *The Trail to Golden Cariboo,* is the story of another amazing journey, from Kamloops to Cameronton, where Archie and his partners had staked their claims and where Cariboo Cameron had found a fortune in gold.

Again, dangers beset the travellers. Disaster threatened when their wagons met a train of camels! It may be hard to believe, but twenty-three camels were actually brought to the Cariboo area as pack animals. Aside from their unfortunate abilities to spook other animals and to fight with them, camels were badly suited to be pack animals in the Cariboo. They could not carry the huge loads the purchasers had hoped; their feet, well adapted to desert travel, were not at all suited to wet, muddy trails, and they readily became infected. Camels were soon banned from the roads and trails. Sadly, some died quickly; some escaped or were turned loose and survived in the wild for a few years. However unpleasant they were, whatever havoc they caused, ill-informed humans were responsible for the camels' misery.

The road went only partway to the mining towns in 1863. Travellers continued by trail. One man wrote, "Our horses were often plunged up to the belly in swamps and mud. British Columbia is truly a horse-killing country." When Lisa's party came to the end of the wagon road, the trail onwards was lined with the decaying corpses of animals that had been mired.

The trip itself was not Lisa's biggest problem, however. Mrs. McNaughton was determined to make a lady out of Lisa, and ladies certainly did not go mining for gold.

What would become of Lisa and her dreams?

CHAPTER N.º 1

Mrs. Bell dragged me along by my ear— my right ear, to be precise. It hurt, but Ma's shocked face hurt even worse after Mrs. Bell had had her say. Was anybody ever as unlucky as I was? Mrs. Bell was the only white woman in Kamloops besides Ma. She was a guest in the factor's home, and she had to catch me!

"Doing laundry on the Sabbath, *Missus* Schubert," she said, looking down her long nose. "In the home of a single man—and him in his underdrawers. Is that how you train your girls?"

"No," said Ma quietly. "Lisa, is this story true?"

My face flamed.

"Do you doubt me?" If Mrs. Bell had been angry before, now she was spitting mad. "Your girl breaks the Sabbath. No doubt, she'll lie as well. What can you expect, taking in orphans?"

"It's true." I gulped and burst into tears.

Ma opened her arms, like always when one of us is hurting, and gathered me in. She talked over my head to Mrs. Bell. "I have to thank you for your information, Mrs. Bell," she said, "though Lisa is not an orphan. She was born our niece, and now she's our daughter, as much as the others. Please go now. Mr. Schubert and I will deal with this."

"She needs a good whipping," said Mrs. Bell, "and I hope she gets it. Spare the rod and spoil the child, Missus Schubert. This girl has no respect for her elders. There'll be worse to come, you mark my words." Her skirts rustled as she turned, and the door slammed shut behind her.

"Tell me, Lisa," said Ma.

"Money to get to the Cariboo," I sobbed. "I

know you and Papa aren't leaving Kamloops, Ma. I heard you talking. So I have to go by myself. I can live with Archie, can't I?"

Papa came home just then. He never has whipped me, but then I've minded him and Ma the best I could since my own papa died. Papa rubbed his spectacles with his handkerchief while he listened.

"Was Mr. Simpson really in his drawers?" Papa was angrier about that than anything. "He's the one should get a beating, and I'm the man to give it. Destroying your reputation, Lisa, and you still a child."

"Papa, what else could he wear?" I asked. "Both his shirts and his two pair of trousers, three pair of socks, and his red flannels—every stitch he owns, I think, was caked with dirt. I've never done such a stinking wash."

Papa's shoulders shook and his face turned red. I trembled for Mr. Simpson. "Papa, don't beat him, please," I begged. "I'll never get more work in this town."

Papa let out a snort and then a great roar of laughter. "I doubt your career as a laundress is going to last, Lisa," he said, "not on the Sabbath. We cannot allow that, and well do you know it."

I had told myself that this was a matter of life and death, the same as when we were on the trail and starving and winter was coming on, when the Sabbath had become a day like any other. But I knew the difference. I wanted to go to the Cariboo. I wanted to go mining and find gold. I wanted to get away from Mrs. Bell and all the others who kept watching me and looking down their noses. I was not about to argue with Papa. But I had to say something, to explain.

"What other time do I have?" I was still crying. "I'll never get to the Cariboo. I'll never find gold and make us rich and send for my trunk from Fort Garry." I snuffled again.

"Most men who go to the Cariboo don't find gold either," said Papa. "It's not lying around everywhere for the taking, Lisa. There is gold, but it's hard to find, and it costs plenty to get it out of the ground after you find it. The stories here are nothing like the ones we heard back home. There's steady work for me here in Kamloops while the Hudson's Bay Company moves the fort to the south side of the river. I need the work, Lisa, with five children to feed. Once I get ahead, I can decide what to do next."

"It's hard for you here, Lisa," said Ma slowly. "More than I knew. Now it will be worse. I will never whip you, but Mrs. Bell won't let it go, I fear. She's only a visitor, but she's a busybody who'll turn others against you. Augustus, what's best to do?"

"It is the Sabbath," said Papa. "Let us bow our heads and ask the good Lord to guide us."

CHAPTER N°2

I do not believe that God sits around in heaven waiting to advise our family. He must have more important things to do. But sometimes I wonder. Surely prayer has never been answered faster: Archie's letter arrived the very next day. Papa brought it when he came home for dinner.

"For me, Papa?" I held out my hand.

"It's addressed to me," said Papa quickly. "But you're a good reader, Lisa. You can read it out to all of us."

My body was all goosebumps as I took the folded paper out of his hand. We'd been in

Kamloops since last October, when baby Rose was born. It was June now. Archie had written once, to say he and all the others were safe, but that was all. I stared at the paper, but I didn't see the words. I saw Archie holding the other side of the pan when we tried to pan for gold, Archie waving goodbye from the raft as the foaming river whirled him out of my sight. Maybe he had found gold already in the Cariboo.

"Is the writing so hard to understand?" Ma asked gently.

I shook my head and began to read.

"It is addressed to Augustus Schubert, Esq., Kamloops," I said.

"What's 'esk'?" my brother Gus demanded.

"That's how one gentleman addresses another," said Ma. "Esquire, it means. Go on, Lisa."

When your whole life depends on a letter, it's hard to read it fast—but you want to read it fast, to know and not know, both at the same time.

"'Dear Mr. Schubert,'" I began. "'It is many months since I have written to you, but I had little news to impart and none good. We were all deceived, except maybe the few who had been mining in California, like Mr. Wattie, yet he has been disappointed too. We have staked our claims, but the gold is not lying in nuggets for the taking. A few miners have struck pay dirt, and me and my partners remain hopeful, but mining is now a costly venture, and in good conscience I cannot advise you to chance it here.'"

"Just what I've heard," Papa muttered.

"'My own circumstances have changed, however,'" the letter went on. "'I am journeying to Victoria to be married. By the time you read this letter, God willing, my cousin Elizabeth McGregor will be my wife.'"

"Elizabeth McGregor." Ma rolled the words around on her tongue. "I cannot recall that he ever mentioned her name."

"'My bride-to-be comes from Montreal,'" I continued. "'We played together as children; we've always cared for each other. When her whole family perished from the fever, I was proud to offer her my hand and the protection of my name.'"

Poor Elizabeth. How awful to lose all your family at once. It was bad enough when my own dear father died. Poor me as well—I had daydreamed of wedding Archie myself when I was grown up. Papa put his big hands gently on my shoulders. I leaned against him; the buttons on his waistcoat pressed into my back.

"Poor girl," he said. I wasn't sure if he meant me or Elizabeth.

"Archie's young," said Ma, "but he's a good man. But why does he write of such personal matters to us?"

My eyes had skimmed further over the letter while they talked. "He wants me to live with them," I blurted out. "Papa, Ma, I can go mining after all."

Ma's mouth opened, but no words came out. Papa took off his spectacles and set them on the table. Baby Rose chose this moment to start screaming, setting her cradle jiggling to and fro.

Jamie and Mary Jane began to cry as well. Gus just looked at me.

I love Ma and Papa and all the children. They are my family. But I want to be a miner. I want to go to the Cariboo.

"Jamie, Mary Jane, stop that racket," Ma commanded. She picked up the baby and took her behind the curtain to nurse. "Go on reading, Lisa."

"'My bride is a gentlewoman,'" Archie had written. "'She knows nothing of frontier ways and the life of a mining camp. I have prepared for her as best I can, but I fear that our rude accommodations and way of life will be a hardship. Indeed, I intended to make our home in Victoria and to spend the winters there. However, my fortunes do not yet permit of this, and my Elizabeth says she wishes to share my life, and that rude quarters will be the better for a lady's presence.

"'I could hire an Indian woman to help in the house,'" he went on, "'but she wouldn't speak our language much, and her ways would not be ours. Lisa is young, but she is a smart girl and a good worker. If you will entrust her to us, my wife will train her in housewifely duties, and we will further her education. We will expect her to help in the house and in the garden that my wife intends to plant. Lisa will be company for my wife during the hours and days I must be gone.'"

"I told you," taunted Gus. "Girls can't go mining. Archie only wants you to help in the house."

"Enough," Papa snapped. "Gus, help Lisa get dinner on the table. I must get back to work. We'll talk about this tonight."

CHAPTER N.º 3

So that is why Papa and I were tramping along the trail towards the Bonaparte River, where the new wagon road to the Cariboo snaked its way north. Mr. Donald McLean and his sons had built a stopping house at Hat Creek, and that's where Papa's letter had said we'd meet Archie and his wife.

What a difference from our journey downriver to Kamloops last October! At the end of that trip, we were crowded onto a raft, cold, wet, and almost starving. It was the middle of June now, and all the snow had melted. Papa whistled a tune as we walked, and I joined in.

Gus and his teasing hadn't spoiled my happiness. Most likely Archie only said things about housework and keeping his wife company so my folks would let me come. He knew I didn't like girls' jobs around the house; he knew I wanted to be a miner. I felt bad about deceiving Papa and Ma, but I could do some housework and lots of mining too.

Papa led a borrowed mule, since we had neither horse nor cart of our own. The mule carried a leather bag on each side, one packed with clothes and blankets, the other, with food and water for us and oats for the mule, as well as a few keepsakes. Our prospecting pan, the only piece of mining gear we'd saved when our raft broke up in the river, was tied on the mule's back, and the whole load was held together with a diamond hitch. After a winter in town, my legs ached and my feet burned when I'd walked for only a few hours. I didn't feel like whistling any more.

"I've gotten soft," I said in disgust when we stopped to make camp. "I used to walk all day, and I didn't get blisters."

"You'll toughen up quicker than before," Papa told me. "You did get blisters at first, after we left Fort Garry."

The fur-trade trail was well used and clear enough, though we had to go around many ancient stumps where giant fir trees had been cut down; rotting logs still lay to each side where they had fallen.

"The fastest route is the one where you won't get lost," Papa said. "I hear there's a shorter way to the wagon road than we're taking, but it's not well marked."

"This is fine," I told him. I threw back my bonnet and let the sun warm my yellow hair. Ma would have made me put it on again, but Papa wouldn't notice and wouldn't care if he did. The trail was dry, the mud well packed between the stumps and rocks—and, joy of joys, there were no mosquitoes! I asked Papa why not?

"It's dry; there are no swampy places for the pests to breed." Papa grinned. "Better than a year ago, isn't it? I thought the mosquitoes would carry you away in the night!"

Giant trees and rocky cliffs sometimes reminded me of our struggle when we set out from Tête Jaune Cache to Kamloops, where there had been no trail at all. This was better. Though I stumbled often and fell a few times, I never hurt myself enough to notice. Papa was not so lucky. When he fell, on the afternoon of our third day, he got up fast enough, but he walked slower and favoured his left leg.

"We should stop," I told him. "Let me bind up your foot."

It was hard to pull off his leather boot. I clambered down to the river and filled our prospecting pan—luckily, the slope was not too steep. Papa soaked his swollen foot while I built a fire and fried up some bacon and beans. "Looks worse than it is," Papa said. "I'll be right as rain come morning."

He cut himself a stout stick first thing next morning, and another one for me, and on we went. We rested more often that day. Papa may have gritted his teeth a few times, but he did not limp.

Suddenly, we came round a bend in the trail. A green valley stretched in front of us, rolling gently down to a stream that sparkled in the sun. Half a dozen black cattle lifted their heads to look at us, then went back to their grazing. The mule pulled Papa forward, and Papa laughed and let go of the rope so that the animal could get at the good grass. Near the stream stood a log house, much like our house in Kamloops, but bigger and newer, the huge logs still fresh and raw. I could see horses in a corral and two enormous wagons standing near the house.

"Archie will be waiting for us," I said.

"Maybe, if our letter reached him," Papa replied.

"Oh, Papa! How awful if it didn't!"

"I sent it to Victoria with Father Pandosy, from the mission," said Papa. "I'm sure he'd do his best. Well, run on down, Lisa. I can see you're itching to go."

CHAPTER N.º 4

I hoisted my skirts and raced down the hill. "Archie!" I shouted.

A gentleman jumped up from a long trestle table set up out back of the house. Archie? In black trousers and waistcoat and a high-collared white shirt? I'd never seen Archie wear anything but a flannel shirt and thick woollen workman's trousers, even in summer. I'd have pulled back, except I was running too hard. But Archie hadn't changed. He caught me in his arms and swung me around, then set me down. I stood back a little.

"How you've grown," he said admiringly. "Put flesh on your bones too. You aren't the scrawny waif I left at Tête Jaune Cache."

"Mr. McNaughton!" A lady dressed in black silk stared at Archie, who turned as red as a beet. "Will you be so kind as to introduce this young person?" Her face was like fine china, pale and rigid, under a plain black velvet bonnet; she did not get up from the table to greet us.

My heart sank as I realized who she must be. Archie stammered, "My dear, this is my young friend Lisa Schubert. Pardon our unmannerly greeting, my love. When we parted, we did not know if either of us would survive, or if we should ever meet again. Lisa, this lady is my wife. I'm sure you'll be good friends."

I almost laughed out loud. Friends! He had changed after all and not for the better. I glared at him. Then I bobbed my head towards her. "Pleased to meet you, ma'am," I said. My voice was small. My face burned with mingled rage and shame. Would they want to take me, after so

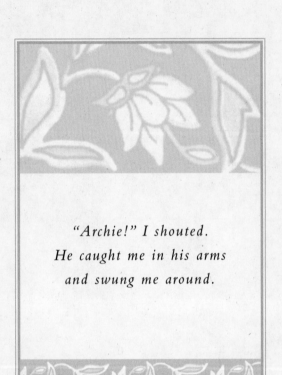

"Archie!" I shouted.
He caught me in his arms
and swung me around.

bad a beginning? *Would I want to go?*

Papa arrived as the lady made some reply. I hardly heard her, nor did I hear much of what the grown-ups said, being sunk in my own misery. Vaguely, I recall somebody bringing chairs for Papa and me, and dishes of stew with green peas and fresh beans and beef, and fresh-baked bread for dipping in the gravy. It was the best meal put before me in months. Papa came back for seconds, and I gave him mine.

"You're too excited to eat," Papa chuckled, beaming at Archie and his wife.

I couldn't look at her. Some ladies back east, some gentlemen too, called each other Mr. and Mrs. in public, and for all I knew in private too, but Ma and Papa called each other "Ma" and "Papa," just like us children. Long ago, on the trail, Archie had told me not to call him Mr. McNaughton—but how could I address him more familiarly than his own wife did? Mrs. Bell's nose was nowhere near as long as Mrs. Archibald McNaughton's.

She looked down her nose at the log house too. "Hat Creek Ranch!" she sniffed. "Sounds important, like Ashcroft Manor, and they're nobbut log huts with dirt floors, both of them, and everybody sleeps on the floor, and there's nary a chamber pot to be seen, nor any private place indoors to use it, only a stinking privy out the back." She ran out of steam at the same time she ran out of breath.

The owner of Hat Creek Ranch, Mr. McLean, had been chief factor for the Hudson's Bay Company at Fort Kamloops before he retired. We had not met him, but Papa knew all the men at the fort, and the McLean family gathered around us to catch up on the news.

Archie's party had arrived only the day before, so we had timed our meeting well; however, Mrs. McNaughton refused to make her bed again on the floor in company with a crowd of miners. "Such snoring, Mr. Schubert; I didn't catch a wink. Mr. McNaughton and I propose to sleep tonight in the wagon."

"Under the stars, I suspect, madam," said Papa. "If it doesn't come on to rain, you'll do very well." He offered his arm as Mrs. McNaughton finally stood up. She didn't exactly stand, though; she glided. My mouth fell open. The lady was wearing enormous hoops under her long black skirt, which billowed out around her like a sail. I hadn't seen hooped skirts since Fort Garry, and then only for Sundays, and never as big as these. Papa adjusted his arm as best he could to give her room. He smiled down at the china face. "It's a long time since I've had a fine lady on my arm," he said. "I doubt you'll be comfortable in the open. Shall we pitch a tent, Archie? Lisa and I will help."

"The stars will do well enough, thank you," said the lady. "I mean to be a frontier wife and must learn frontier ways." Archie beamed at her.

"That's the spirit," Papa said. It was colder in the open than on the trail, but Papa and I rolled up snug in our blankets and slept. Maybe all would be well.

CHAPTER N° 5

Eavesdropping is sneaky, but when two people talk loud enough that you can't help but hear them, what's to do but lie quiet and keep your ears peeled? Especially when they're talking about you.

"Poor child, any good Christian woman would pity her." That was Mrs. McNaughton's voice.

"She's a sunny lass and a braw worker, my love," said Archie. "She's not to blame that she worked alongside men on the long trek overland and picked up some of our rough manners. Full of spunk, she is—saved her brother's life, and her

24

own too, when their raft broke up in the rapids."

Rough manners! Did Archie really think that? Ma would be mortified. I was mortified myself and barely heard the next sentence as I burrowed deep into my blankets.

Archie's wife said, "Manners can be learned. It will be my duty to teach her."

Duty is an ugly word, a word without kindness or love. One of the sentences for practice in Ma's old penmanship book said, "I slept and dreamed that life was beauty; I woke and knew that life was duty." I never copied that one out, but now I could not get it out of my mind. Papa would surely take me home with him if I asked, but then I'd never get to the Cariboo. And Mrs. McNaughton said she wanted to be a frontier wife.

There was no chance for a serious talk later that morning; I couldn't get Papa off by himself, and I couldn't think what I'd say if I did. Everything was already decided. Archie had hired six men to help him and his partners in the gold-fields; these men and a crowd of other would-be miners were already hurrying through their breakfast at the big outdoor table, everybody in a rush to get to the Cariboo. The smell of bacon made my stomach rumble.

Archie climbed into one of the vast wagons, and Papa slung my bags up for him to stow away. "Is everything in this wagon yours?" Papa asked.

"Everything in this and the other wagon as well," said Archie. "I don't know quite how we'll manage, but my wife sent twice as much as this by sea around the Horn. Mr. Morrow has stored some of her goods in Victoria; this is what she couldn't bear to leave behind. Nobody else will have an organ!"

"You will be the most civilized family in the Cariboo." Papa chuckled.

Archie laughed, a little grimly. "A mahogany table and chairs on a dirt floor," he said. "I hope to build a better house next year, but not unless I can find gold."

I held up my arms for Archie to pull me up to see inside the wagon, but he jumped down and led the way back to his wife. Papa put his arms around me and talked over my shoulder to the McNaughtons. "Take good care of my big girl," he said, and the lady in black from Montreal told him they would take very good care indeed.

Papa took off his spectacles and wiped them on his handkerchief; then he blew his nose. I snuffled myself. We hugged each other for a long time. At last, Papa loosened his arms. "That's my brave girl," he said quietly. Then he turned towards the meadow and started up the hill to the trail to Kamloops, leading the mule.

"Come, Lisa," said the voice of duty, "let me braid your hair while the men pack our blankets."

"I can help them," I said. "Or maybe I should make breakfast."

"We'll take breakfast at the ranch," she said. "Come and sit." Her hands when she brushed my hair were gentle; she worked at the tangles. But she braided my hair so tight my scalp hurt. I looked up at her. "I know it's tight," she said. "It will loosen up, you know."

"Eat your breakfast, Lisa," Mrs. Mac commanded. "The mules are hitched; we must be on our way."

I could walk faster than the wagons moved, even with a team of six mules to pull each of them, but I did not say so. I nibbled, but I can't eat much when somebody is staring at me. At last, Archie called us. His wife glided to her feet. "I'll tell him you're nearly ready," she said. As soon as her back was turned, I piled the rest of my plateful of bacon between two big pieces of bread and butter and sneaked it into my apron pocket.

"Good girl." Mrs. Mac smiled at my empty plate. I guessed I could fool her easily enough, even if fooling her made me feel bad. Ma would have smelled the bacon and known right off what I'd done. But Ma would not have made me eat fast when I couldn't.

Archie held the halter rope for a glossy black mare, a small horse but spirited from the way she held herself, ready to run. I ran over to stroke her velvety nose. "She's beautiful." I gulped. "What's her name? Is she yours, Archie? Can I ride her? Oh, please!"

He laughed. "Her name is Queenie," he said. "Don't you think she's a mite small for me? I bought her for Mrs. McNaughton to ride when we run out of road. Maybe she'll allow you up from time to time. Queenie needs to be exercised. What do you think, my dear?"

"Perhaps," said Mrs. Mac. "Are you a good horsewoman, Lisa?"

"I rode Ma's horse, Star, lots of times," I boasted. "I could help you with Queenie, ma'am. I know how to rub her down after a gallop; it would be a pleasure."

Mrs. Mac glanced down at her hoops. "Yes," she said, "that would be helpful, Lisa. Maybe tomorrow, when we are not so rushed. No gallop-ing, mind you. But I see the mules are harnessed." She gestured to the bench at the front of the wagon, where the driver sat, reins in hand. "Up you go," she said. "Duncan, give Lisa a hand."

Duncan, the driver, nodded cheerfully. Like most of the men, he sported a red flannel shirt. From his barrel shoulders and arms like tree trunks, I thought he must be a big man and was surprised later to see he was not much taller than I was, though in every other way he was big—and very strong, as I immediately found out. "Hang on, girlie," he said, holding out a looped rope on the end of a stick; then he lifted me up, dangling like a parcel, though he held me carefully away from the wheel so my yellow gingham dress and my good petticoat could not pick up dirt.

"I won't go up that way," said Mrs. Mac. "Mr. McNaughton, assist me, if you please."

If I couldn't ride Queenie, I wanted to walk with Archie, but I could see this was no time to ask. Besides, I'd never sat so high up. I could see for miles and miles—maybe that was the river in the distance, the Bonaparte. It would be too bad to get soft again, but I could walk another day.

"If we have to off-load the wagons, we'll spend the day getting across the river," Archie grumbled. "It's a pity they didn't build the main road on this side all the way."

"No need to fret," said Duncan. "You'll see." He picked up his reins and called softly, and our wagon lurched forward as all six mules began to pull.

Mrs. McNaughton's hoops squashed me on one side, and Duncan squashed me on the other, like the bacon in my sandwich. "Is it hard to walk with such wide hoops?" I asked.

She turned bristly again. "You should address me as Mrs. McNaughton, or ma'am," she said, "and it is not polite for a young person to ask such a personal question. In a few years, you will be old enough yourself for a dress with hoops. Meanwhile, you must have a proper crinoline, Lisa. I shall find a seamstress to make one for you."

"That is kind of you, ma'am." But how could I go mining in a crinoline? How could I do housework? How could I mount a horse? "I think it must be difficult to make a fire in the stove, or stir the soup pot, or even sweep the floor in a crinoline," I said. And hoops! Mrs. Mac's hoops were so wide she had to turn sideways to get through the door into the house. I hated hoops.

Mrs. Mac looked down her long nose and turned away. Fine. Now I could talk to Duncan. He turned out to be a Metis man, like many in Kamloops. His mother was an Indian, his father a trader for the Hudson's Bay. He had an Indian name too, but he said Duncan was easier.

"Have you been driving big wagons for a long time?" I asked. "Have you always lived here? Have you been to the Cariboo, all the way?"

I could feel Mrs. Mac sniffing. I was afraid she would tell me that ladies did not have conversations with wagon drivers. She had not told me yet, though. Before Duncan got far with answers, we rounded a curve, and there was the river. Our road wound through green meadows down the hill. Duncan set the brake to help slow the wagon, and the sure-footed mules took us down to the dock and the waiting ferry.

"I've never seen a boat like that," I said. "Why is it tied up?" Above the ferry, a massive cable led from one shore to the other. I thought I could see pulleys. The boat—more like a barge—was attached to the cable.

"The current takes us across," said Duncan, "and back too, when we're ready. We will unharness the mules. It's safer, in case of accident. But I've never had an accident here."

Duncan and the ferryman turned something on the bottom of the barge to catch the current, and off we went; they turned the boards the other way, and the current took the empty barge back for the second wagon and mules. In little more than an hour, both wagons were across.

CHAPTER N.º 6

The new wagon road was a marvel, wide enough for two teams to pass. Sometimes our path led across great valleys that had been built up by cribs of gigantic logs filled with rocks. Sometimes the road had been cut through sheer rocky cliffs. Sometimes it dipped almost level with the river, then it would rise until the river was nothing but a silver ribbon far below.

Unfortunately, we met the camel train on a high place.

Camels? I blinked, but they did not disappear. We found out later that an American man had brought in twenty-three of them, at enormous cost (ten times the cost of a good pack horse!) thinking to make his fortune taking goods to the mines.

Unluckily, we had the outside edge of the road. I've never seen anything like the panic, and hope I never do again. It was ten times worse than when Mr. Morrow's ox pulled the cart over the poor man's head on our journey from Fort Garry.

Anybody could see that the mules and the camels hated each other, but the camels were bigger and stronger, and they were not tied to other camels. They bit and kicked; the mules screamed and bucked. Duncan, whip in hand, jumped down and ran to the lead mules, yelling for help. Two more of Archie's men ran forward. I slid over to where Duncan had been sitting. I wanted Mrs. Mac to get down with me, in case the wagon went over the cliff, but Mrs. Mac seemed to have other ideas. She held onto me with one arm and onto the wagon with the other.

At least she did not scream, but she did not pay any attention to me either. Then Archie jumped up beside us, his wife let go, and I was free. I jumped down and ran back, looking for the horse. Those camels—what a stink they made! Queenie pulled loose from where she'd been tied to the wagon just as I reached her. Her eyes were all white and strange. One of the camels landed a kick on her rump. Queenie reared, and her hind feet slipped in the loose shale at the side of the road.

"Queenie," I yelled, "Queenie!" Somehow, I caught her halter; somehow, I chased off the camel. It must have been a funny sight, if anybody could have looked down on it: small me brandishing a frying pan and beating the camel's nose with it while I held Queenie's halter and pulled away from the cliff. I don't know where I got the frying pan. It must have come from the wagon, but I don't remember finding it. It was a big heavy iron pan, but I didn't notice that until afterwards when my arm ached. For sure, there was nothing funny about it at the time.

Next thing I noticed, Mrs. McNaughton had her arms around me, and Archie had hold of Queenie's halter. Mrs. Mac felt as stiff as she looked; her corsets must be full of whalebone, but her arms were strong, almost like Ma's. I was shivering.

"Mr. McNaughton, my dear," she said, "please fetch my fur robe. This child needs warming; she has had a shock."

I looked around, but there was not one camel to be seen. "They've gone," said Mrs. Mac. "Good riddance too. It's nobbut luck we didn't lose a wagon over the cliff. I intend writing to Governor Douglas about those camels. The sooner they go back where they came from, the better." Her dark eyes flashed. For once, there was colour in her china cheeks. Maybe the camels had put me in her good books, at least for that day.

We did get on better afterwards. I rode between her and Duncan, or walked with Archie and the men he had hired. When the wagons had to turn

It must have been a funny sight: small me brandishing a frying pan and beating the camel's nose with it while I held Queenie's halter.

back, those men would help carry our goods the rest of the way; then they would work on Archie's claim. There were only six men. I wondered how many trips they would have to take to carry everything. Maybe Archie would hire more packers. Maybe Mrs. Mac would leave some things behind.

As we continued, the weather changed. Most days we had some rain. The mosquitoes appeared in their black clouds. Then we were truly thankful for the roadhouses, no matter how rough, and tried to get into shelter well before dusk.

I discovered that the Royal Engineers from the army in England had surveyed the road and built the first part of it. Soon Sergeant McColl and Lance Corporal Turnbull would come to lay out the Williams Creek townsites, including Cameronton, where we were going. "You'll be able to buy a plot of land for building, if you've got the money," Duncan said.

"Mr. McNaughton has built a house already," I said proudly.

Mrs. Mac did not join our talks, but she listened; every now and then, she smiled, like now when Duncan said, "Just as well he has. You'll see the dining table and chairs later, when we take the oilcloth off them. Mahogany wood and shined so bright you can see your face in the tabletop. It'd be a shame to put that table in a tent."

Archie's party had travelled by paddlewheel steamer from New Westminster to Yale, where the wagon road began. "I guess they've finished the wagon road maybe as far as 150 Mile by now," Duncan said, "though that's still a weary way from Cameronton."

"Why is it called 150 Mile?" Duncan didn't care if I asked questions.

Duncan laughed. "It don't make much sense," he said. "The short answer is, it's that many miles from Lillooet; but Lillooet's on the old road, Governor Douglas's old road, not on this new wagon road at all. There's 70 Mile, 100 Mile, 108 Mile, 150 Mile, and plenty more in between on this road, so when you get to one of them, you know how far you've come from the last."

Nobody could tell us exactly how far the road had been built, except that it ended a long way before Cameronton, near where Archie and his partners had staked their claims and where Archie had built his house.

"I helped pack out Sophia Cameron's coffin last winter," Duncan said. "Coldest trip I ever made and the nastiest. Cariboo paid twelve dollars a day, with a two thousand dollar bonus if you stuck it out all the way to Victoria. I stayed with him and his partner until we got out of the snow; then they bought a horse and cart and paid us off. We started with twenty-two men; by that time, there were only eight of us left. She was a terrible weight, poor lady. Her husband—John Duncan is his name, but everybody calls him Cariboo, on account of how much gold he's found—he had the tinsmith make her coffin, and he filled it with alcohol, so her body wouldn't rot."

"Duncan, that's enough!" Mrs. McNaughton's voice was like ice, though I was sure she found this story as fascinating as I did. I was lucky that Duncan got to tell that much of it. Perhaps Archie would tell me more.

However, Archie couldn't or wouldn't tell me much. Sophia had died of the mountain fever. "Poor lady, she died on a cold day last October, cold enough to freeze the tears on your face. It was typhoid, I believe," Archie said. "Any kind of fever here, most folks say it's the mountain fever. There was a lot of typhoid last year, starting soon after we Overlanders arrived. We lived on our claims and tried to stay away from town. People aren't allowed to throw garbage into the creek any more, and we're going to build a hospital. This season will be better, but still I worry about my wife. I'm glad you will be with her, Lisa."

We were walking in drizzling rain. In my blanket coat that Ma had made, I smelled wet and woolly, like a sheep.

"I want to come mining with you, Archie," I said. "Have you forgotten?"

"I hoped *you* would forget." Archie shook his head. "I should have known better, Lisa. Well, my dear, we'll see, but that may not be possible." He looked at me anxiously.

I burst into tears. How could I not? My dearest wish, and now it might never come true.

"Oh, Lisa!" Archie's sad voice set me to crying even harder. Before he was married, Archie would have hugged me; now he took my hand, and we walked together. I tried not to make any noise, though big tears mingled with the rain on my cheeks. After a while, I pulled out my handkerchief and blew my nose. Then I went back to the wagon. I did not feel like walking with Archie any more.

Sophia Cameron had held a claim, Duncan told me when we stopped for dinner; she had often gone out to the diggings with her husband, though she died two months before the Cameron Mining Company made its big strike. A few other women did the same.

"Only three or four that I've seen, though," said Duncan, "and there must be two or three thousand men there now and more arriving every day. If you dress like a boy, though, Lisa, and pin your hair under a cap, you'll be fine. I'll never tell!" He winked at me.

I felt a little better, but not much. What would Mrs. Mac say if I dressed like a boy? Nothing good, for sure.

CHAPTER *N°* 7

The next day was sunny and warm, but I still felt miserable and sat hunched on the wagon with nothing to say. Mrs. Mac tried three times, but questions about my family or home in Kamloops only made me want to cry again. Finally, she said, "Lisa, I know you would like to ride Queenie. Get down, girl, and tell Mr. McNaughton I wish him to saddle her for you."

"Really, ma'am?"

"Really." She laughed. "It's been mean of me not to let you ride after you saved her life, but truly, Lisa, I had hoped for flat land. As far as I can see, this road is all hills, valleys, and cliffs. However, my husband tells me you ride well, so go and ride. Meanwhile, I'll think of something else for you to do. I do not care for this moping about."

Archie laughed when I found him. "I'm glad," he said. "A ride will do you good, and Queenie too. Have you ridden sidesaddle, Lisa?"

"Never." I gulped. "Ma always used a man's saddle. She wore trousers when we left St. Paul. She could ride faster that way, and she wasn't worried about falling off. For our Overland trip, she cut a skirt in two pieces. When she stood up, it looked like a proper skirt, but she could ride with one leg on each side, and that's how I ride too."

"My saddle will have to do then," said Archie. "I can dig it out easily enough, but Queenie won't like it, it's so big and heavy."

"Can't I ride bareback?" I asked. "I've done that plenty of times."

"A packsaddle would be better," said Archie. "It's only a bag full of straw, but I can cinch it; it would give you something to grab if you start to slip. My wife won't be happy about this, I'm afraid," said Archie. He shrugged. "You're a child still. If your pantaloons show, it's no great matter. Queenie knows you. I think you can manage her with a packsaddle. Keep a firm hand on the reins, though, Lisa; we don't want any runaways."

Queenie was the perfect name for the black mare. With me securely on her back, she pranced delicately past the walkers, past the wagons and the mules. Queenie liked leading the procession. I liked it too. We would both have liked to gallop, but I held her back. "Good girl, Queenie, we'll walk or trot today. Tomorrow we'll go faster," I told her. I was sure she understood.

"You smell of horse," said Mrs. Mac later. "Why didn't you ask Mr. McNaughton to help get out your riding clothes? Has nobody taught you to ride like a lady?" She shook her head, but she was smiling, not looking down her nose; it made a big difference.

"I don't have special clothes for riding," I said, "except for a pair of Papa's old trousers that Ma cut down for me, but I thought you would not like me to wear them, ma'am. But, oh, please let me ride Queenie again tomorrow. I'll wash my dress and my petticoat and my pantaloons and stockings every time."

"Get yourself into the back of the wagon and change now," said Mrs. Mac. "It's not proper, Lisa. 'Begin as you mean to go on,' is my motto, and that does not mean permitting you to ride like a boy." She sighed.

Or dress like a boy, I thought.

No mining, no riding—my world was gloomy in the next few days. The weather, cold and rainy, and windy too, did nothing to cheer me up. There wasn't much to see, except fog and cloud. Mrs. Mac sat silently beside Duncan, but I crept under the canvas top of the wagon, although the rain found places to come in, by drips and rivulets. Everything in the wagon was tied up in oilcloth; I hoped the rain would not find any holes in it.

My real mama died on the ship coming to America when I was born. She would have let me go mining. Likely she would have gone mining herself. We could have found gold together! I wiggled, trying to find a place where sharp corners of furniture tied up in oilcloth did not poke into me. "Mama," I sobbed, "I wish you had not died." For a moment, I could almost see her, looking like me but older, with bright eyes and yellow curls twisted into a knot on top of her head. Nobody had ever made a picture of her, but my father had told me what she looked like lots of times before he died in St. Paul, before my aunt and uncle and their children became my family.

The most dreadful homesickness took hold of me. Ma had given me one of her old aprons; it still smelled like our kitchen in Kamloops. I buried my head in its white folds and sobbed.

I didn't think anyone could hear me, but I was wrong.

"So, Lisa is feeling sorry for herself." Mrs. Mac's voice was brisk and bracing. "We must have a project, you and I. Let us observe the plants as we pass. It will be your job to pick one of each kind—better, pull up the whole plant, with the roots. I will lend you an apron with deep pockets. When your pockets are full, come back to the wagon and we'll study what you have found."

I had never liked working in the garden, though I had pulled plenty of weeds, helping Ma. "I don't want to," I said, then, quickly, "Please, ma'am, I'd rather not."

"Stop whining, girl. By the time we reach the Cariboo, you'll have your own botanical collection. We have wasted time. I have been remiss. Now you must apply yourself to your education. It is your duty to learn and mine to teach you."

Boring plants. But every time I pulled up a plant, I looked for rock with yellow glitter. Once I ran to show Archie, shivering with excitement.

He shook his head. "Fool's gold," he said. "The real thing is a softer yellow, not as glittery as this, and don't expect to see much of it. Keep looking, though, Lisa, and show me what you find."

"Good," I said. "I'll know what gold looks like when I find it." Archie did not reply.

I rubbed down Queenie every night. I talked to her, and she as good as talked to me, nickering softly. Archie and I made sure that Queenie had water and pasture, and shelter from the rain, if any shelter could be found. One good thing: the mosquitoes disappeared; likely it was too cold for them.

One roadhouse was much like another: full of men who had not washed or changed their clothes for much too long, blue with smoke from pipes and cigars, and from the open fire. We ate beans and bacon for supper and again for breakfast, though once the wife had made fresh bread, and we were in time to buy some before it was gone. I shared a thick slice with Mrs. Mac and spread my half with bacon dripping, since there was no butter. "Bacon dripping is good," I told her, but she did not try it. I wondered if Mrs. Mac would always insist on Montreal ways, or if she would ever understand that frontier life was different.

Sometimes there were two attic rooms for sleeping; sometimes there was only one downstairs room and no attic at all. After we ate, the trestle tables were taken down, and everybody slept on the floor. We did not try to put up a tent in the rain and wind, and I was glad about that. I had slept often enough in a leaky tent on the trip from Fort Garry. Archie made sure that his wife and I had dry places on the roadhouse floor.

When the sun finally came out, we decided to stay an extra day to dry out clothes and bedding. It seemed like a fine day for my laundry business. I asked for the fire to be lit under the big boiler and for a man to keep filling it. We had two boilers in Kamloops, but at the roadhouse they had only one, though there was a big washtub. I set to work.

Mrs. Mac had caught a cold; she coughed a lot and spoke as sharply as she'd done that first day. "Is there nobody else who can use a scrub board?" she demanded. "You'll ruin your hands, Lisa, with that lye soap."

I was washing her white embroidered petti-coats at the time and was about to start on a pile of her linen handkerchiefs. "It's the same kind of soap as I've always used," I told her. "Why don't you have a rest, ma'am? If you wish, I'll make a mustard plaster for your chest after I'm done here."

I hate mustard plasters myself, but Ma says there's nothing half as good to break up a cough. There was goose grease in one of my bags, mustard too, and I knew where to find flour to mix in, so the mustard wouldn't burn. Mrs. Mac had delicate skin; I'd use a double thickness of flannel.

"Mustard plaster?" she said. "That's for children, Lisa. If I had Friar's Balsam, I'd heat some and breathe the vapour." She looked at me hopefully, but I shook my head.

When she had gone, I sighed with relief. Today was not the Sabbath, but Mrs. McNaughton would not want me washing men's underwear, I could be sure of that. It must be hard to do anything, when so many things are not proper.

It was a good day for me. I added four dollars to my purse and only stopped when it was getting too late for the clean clothes to dry. The bushes were loaded with red shirts, grey or brown trousers, and cream-coloured underwear. I folded the laundry as it dried; I did not plan to iron anything. Even if there was a sadiron to heat on the stove at the roadhouse, I saw no ironing table and no place to set one up.

The next day was not good, however. The soap must have been different from our soap at home. My hands were red and burning all over. Just when I'd hoped to ride Queenie again, since all my clothes were clean. Maybe I could even try the sidesaddle, but not until my hands didn't hurt so much. Mrs. Mac found some sweet-smelling lotion. It did not make my hands feel much better, but it smelled a lot better than the bacon grease I would have used.

We had been ten days on the wagon road and reached 150 Mile when something horrible happened. A missionary priest, Father Grandidier, arrived at suppertime on his way to the Cariboo. The day had again been cold and rainy, and the miners who crowded into the one room had drunk too much whiskey. Father Grandidier unrolled his blanket near the fire and knelt to say his prayers.

The miners laughed at him and roared out insults. "D'ya want us to send ya to God?" one of them yelled. He pretended he was going to kick the priest into the fire—at least I hope he was only pretending. I remembered how Ma had hated the whiskey trade in Fort Garry. Men can be disgusting when they are drunk.

Archie stood up, Duncan too. "Enough of that," said Archie, loud and stern. But half a dozen miners shook their fists at him, ready to start a fight.

Just then, the owner rushed in from the kitchen, a revolver in his hand. "Who wants a bullet?" he roared. "I'll put one through the next man who laughs."

He stared at the miners. One by one, they dropped their eyes. There was no more drinking that night. Everyone rolled out their beds, and soon the sound of snoring filled the room.

The miners were slow getting up the next day. The owner had to roust some of them out of their blankets so he could set up the tables for breakfast. Father Grandidier left very early, on horseback, and our wagons were on the road before eight. Mrs. McNaughton sat beside me in silence. I wondered if she was sorry she had not stayed in Victoria.

There was no wind that day, and the sun shone bright and warm, so it was a surprise to hear the sound of thunder. "Where is the storm?" I asked.

Duncan laughed. "That's blasting, not thunder," he said. "I'll be leaving you soon. We're running out of road."

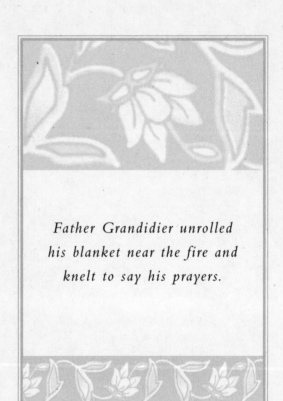

Father Grandidier unrolled his blanket near the fire and knelt to say his prayers.

"Really?"

"Yep. Lookit that rock face. Blasted out no more than a week ago, or I miss my guess."

"How can you be so sure?"

He laughed. "Mainly because we've been travelling over road that wasn't here when I went south a month ago," he said. "Look at that rock face, Lisa: It's clean, nothing growing there. Oh, yes, and you can see the blast marks, where the miners set the powder."

"What happens now? Are we nearly there?"

"Not hardly," Duncan said. "The end of the road is where I turn back, after I unload my wagons, of course, and after Mr. McNaughton settles up. Don't look so worried, Lisa. Mr. McNaughton has hired the most famous packer in the Cariboo to take his goods the rest of the way; he is called Cataline. He'll be here to meet us."

We listened to the thuds of the blasting for several hours; at last, it stopped. The mules' feet on the road and the creaking wagons sounded loud in the sudden silence. "The crew has quit for the day," Duncan said. "They'll share their fire with us, or Cataline will. We'll sleep under the stars tonight."

The sun was low in the sky when we rounded a bend and saw—joyful sight—a lush valley and a trail winding down to a good-sized stream. Beside the stream stood three small tents, like white tipis against the deep green grass.

I wanted to grab hold of Mrs. Mac's arm but managed to hold back. "Please, ma'am, can I run ahead?"

"I expect you *can* run, but that's the wrong question."

I stared at her. What did she mean?

The corners of her mouth turned up in the barest hint of a smile. "The right question is, '*May* I?' and my answer, Lisa, is, 'Yes, you may.'"

"Yes" was all I needed to hear. Archie came up to the wagon as Duncan brought his six mules to a stop, and I jumped down into his arms before I even thought. "Sorry, ma'am," I called back over my shoulder as I pelted down the hill.

Several men looked curiously at me; they were seated, leaning against stumps or logs near a blazing campfire. The carcasses of three small animals roasted over the coals. They hung from a metal rod that was balanced on big rocks. A giant of a man turned the spit. "Are you Cataline?" I asked.

"I am," he replied. "Who, may I ask, are you?"

I introduced myself, and he shook my hand gravely.

Cataline was shaped like an upside-down pear, with huge shoulders and a small waist. Most miners wore red shirts, but Cataline's shirt was white and stiff with starch, although it had no collar. The big man had tied a triangle of light blue silk around his neck instead.

Archie and Mrs. Mac arrived, and the rest of our group, and everything was a bustle of noisy chatter. The tents belonged to the road crew; Cataline and his two men slept in the open, near their mules.

Archie set a cushion against a log and helped his wife arrange her skirts. He seated himself beside her and turned to the big packer. "I hear there's a steamer, *The Enterprise,* that cuts fifty miles off the trip," he said.

"Not exactly," said Cataline. "In a month or two, the road will run as far as Soda Creek, and then you might take the steamer and unload at the end of her run. That is fifty miles, right enough, though you'd still need packers at the end of it. But where the river goes—and the boat—isn't where you want to go. No indeed. You'd have to load and unload two extra times, and you might save twenty, maybe thirty miles. No, take my advice and do it once. My route goes by Stanley and Van Winkle, up Lightning Creek to Jack of Clubs then down Mink Gulch, coming in from the south. I'll get you there sooner by at least two days."

Stanley and Van Winkle, Lightning Creek, Mink Gulch, and Jack of Clubs: I rolled the names around on my tongue. Cataline made them sound like a poem.

"Can you take everything in one trip?" asked Archie.

"I'll have to look at your goods," Cataline admitted. "I'll tell you tomorrow." He took a mouth organ out of his pocket and began to play a jolly, bouncing song. It was in French, and I knew the chorus but not the verses. One of Cataline's men sang, Cataline played, and everybody came in on the chorus, *"En roulant, ma boule roulant, en roulant, ma boule."*

The song went on for a long time. When it was done, Archie started "The Skye Boat Song," all about Prince Charles in Scotland, "the lad that's born to be king." To my surprise, Mrs. Mac joined in. It's a beautiful song, but very sad, about the prince escaping after a dreadful battle. I felt like crying when their voices died away. Then Cataline started "Alouette," and we were all singing and laughing again.

The next day, Cataline took a careful look and said he was pretty certain he could manage in one trip; he'd know for sure when his mules and all the men had packs on their backs.

I cannot tell what the river route would have

been like, but our trail through the woods was hard going indeed. Trees had been cut, but the stumps were left in the ground, and mules and men had churned the mud between them into soupy holes. I kept sinking past my ankles.

The grown-ups sank even deeper until Cataline made everybody cut sticks with sharp points and poke them into the mud to find shallow places to walk. Walking through the mud was bad enough, but plenty of dead bodies of mules and horses lay by the roadside, some standing, still stuck in the mud holes where they had died. My stomach heaved with the smell as well as the sight of them.

Mrs. Mac rode Queenie for a short time, but the poor animal kept floundering. Mrs. Mac wore a black velvet riding skirt with a white blouse and a jacket; she kept looking at the horse and then at her outfit. As soon as we came to a place where the trail was stony and dry, she dismounted. "Mr. McNaughton, please go on ahead," she told Archie. "Take the men, and see that nobody looks back. I have a wash cotton dress in my bag and the boots you bought for me. Lisa, please help me to change."

The "wash cotton" dress was a dainty muslin, light blue and sprigged with white daisies. "I should not be wearing a coloured dress," Mrs. Mac said. "I am still in mourning for my family. However, Queenie may die if I keep riding her, and I can't walk well in my other clothes."

"It's such a pretty dress," I said. "I know you're sad about your family, ma'am, but aren't you tired of wearing black?"

"Tired of doing my duty?" said Mrs. Mac. "No—but it's also my duty to look after Queenie." She smiled. "Mr. McNaughton has not seen this dress," she said.

Mrs. Mac wore ruffled petticoats with her riding costume, but nothing as bulky as a crinoline or hoops. I helped her pack her black velvet into the saddlebag.

Poor Queenie. I could feel her tremble. I wanted to fetch oats and let her rest, but Mrs. Mac said we must not delay the others. I patted Queenie's velvety nose, and Mrs. Mac and I walked on together, leading her. I had not seen Mrs. Mac walk for any distance, but she set a fair pace until the mud got deep again, and then everybody, people and animals, moved slow as snails.

The trail was still littered with dead mules and horses; sometimes vultures pecked at them. Does anything smell fouler than decaying flesh? For a while, I tied a handkerchief over my nose, trying to cut out the stink, but it didn't help much, and it made it hard to breathe. Finally, I took off the kerchief and took quick, shallow breaths, holding my nose. At last, our trail led us out of the muddy stumps, though the smell of decay lingered, sweet and nasty in my nose.

We made camp in a grassy field by a quick-silvery stream. Cataline told us that he had planned his days so that we could reach a good stopping place every night. "We're heavy loaded on this trip," he said, "but we'll make it, you'll see. Now if you folks with nothing to carry want to walk ahead, I expect you can make better time and reach a roadhouse every night." He looked doubtfully at Mrs. Mac.

"If it suits you, Mr. McNaughton," she told her husband, "let us stay with our people and our goods."

"Certainly, my dear." I wished Archie would look at me the way he looked at her right then. It was easy to see he liked the muslin dress.

Mrs. Mac had left her big mahogany table and some other heavy furniture where we unloaded the wagons. I still hadn't seen the shining table-top, as oilcloth still covered everything. Cataline would take the furniture to the steamer and ship it to Quesnel Mouth, to be stored. By next year, maybe, the road would be finished to Cameronton and a wagon could deliver everything. Mrs. Mac refused to leave her little organ behind, however. Two men struggled to carry it. They had made a sort of stretcher and tied the organ on top, still wrapped in oilcloth. At first, Mrs. Mac had put her hand over her eyes every time they almost dropped the stretcher, but after a while, she didn't bother any more.

We caught up to other pack trains, but our mules could not pass them; the trail was too narrow and as nasty as before. I slumped along. "Why not gather more botanical specimens, Lisa?" said Mrs. Mac.

"With dead mules all around?" I was horrified.

"No," she said dryly. "I suggest that you avoid the dead mules."

Ma and Papa don't know much botany. Later, Mrs. Mac told me I had found Indian Paintbrush; it had not blossomed, but the narrow leaves were tipped with red. An open hillside blazed with a bright yellow shrub, too big to pull out by its roots and full of prickles. "Gorse," said Mrs. Mac, "or so I believe, from my books. Gorse does not grow in the east."

I knew the purple vetch flowers, like pea blossoms. "If you can find more of that, Queenie will be happy to eat it," said Mrs. Mac. "Mix it with her oats." Maybe botany was some use after all.

Luckily, everybody on the trail was going to the Cariboo. "There will be as many coming back later," said Cataline. "Some will go to Victoria for the winter and then come back to the mines, but plenty will just give up."

Even though June was almost over, there were still piles of dirty snow, not on the trail, but in the woods and canyons. "We're a mite early," said Cataline. "Two weeks from now, we'd have better going. Not much better, mind you; if it don't snow, it sure does rain."

We pressed on, however, and crossed the south fork of the Quesnel River by ferry, stopping that night at the village of Quesnel Forks. You can buy supplies there, and in the morning Mrs. Mac took me to look at dress goods while the mules were being loaded. We saw some checked gingham—a bolt of blue and white, and another of pink—but Mrs. Mac shook her head. "It's ten times what I'd pay in Montreal," she told the shopkeeper, a stout woman in a plain grey dress and an apron that had once been white, "and poor flimsy stuff at that."

"You're not in Montreal, nor in Victoria neither," said the woman. "If you've come from there, you'll know it's a weary way. Packing alone costs a dollar for every pound."

"It is a hard trip," Mrs. Mac agreed. "However, I won't buy shoddy stuff. Lisa's new dress will have to wait." I blinked.

"I have a good dress," I said stiffly. "Thank you, ma'am. I don't need another."

I patted the crisp gingham and tried not to be spitting mad, although I was. Why did Mrs. Mac tell me she was thinking of me only when she had made up her mind not to buy? The soft blue would be perfect with my yellow hair. It was true that I had a good dress, but not a pretty one. Ma had cut down her brown silk to make me a costume for the Sabbath, a lady's dress with a frill at the neck and another at the bottom of the wide skirt. She had made it big so that I could grow into it. Even holding up my full skirts, I knew that dress would trip me if I tried to run. Sometimes I would have liked to take a pair of scissors and cut the ugly thing to bits, but it had belonged to Ma, and she had made it over especially for me. Ma did not want me beholden to Mrs. Mac.

"All things come to him who waits, Lisa," said Mrs. Mac.

"Yes, ma'am," I said, though I think it's silly to sit around and wait; and I am not a "him."

The mules were loaded. I walked with Cataline. We squelched through mud again, following the east bank of the north fork of the river. Towards noon, we came to a rough bridge. "Spanish Creek," said Cataline. "We have to pay to go across."

"We have to pay on a ferry," I said, "but why on a bridge?"

"We're helping pay for the bridge," said Cataline. "Mr. McNaughton, let me arrange the price. It's cheaper that way."

Soon we were across. On the west side, the trail was not as muddy, but it started to climb, so it was just as tiring. We came to another village, Keithley Creek. "Now you are in the Cariboo," Cataline told me.

I stared at the creek. "Can I pan for gold?" I asked him.

"If we stopped, you could," he said, grinning at me. "I hear a man can take fifteen to twenty dollars a day at Goose Creek, four miles or so that way," he pointed behind us and to the east. "That's good money. The Chinese are moving in there, I believe, but most miners are looking for a fortune, and the fortunes are farther north."

Now we took a mountain trail. Archie's miners groaned, though Cataline and his men carried heavier loads, and the mules heavier still. I stopped looking at the organ. If it was smashed, I didn't want to see. At last, we descended, though going down was almost as difficult as going up. Cataline strode ahead, and when we came to a little creek, he already had tents set up.

The next day we crossed over Snow Shoe Mountain. Much of the trail was dry, though every little hollow was still full of dirty spring snow. "A month ago we'd have needed snowshoes here," Cataline told me. He pointed down to a green valley far below. "There is our camping ground for the night. Tomorrow it's another hard tramp, but we'll reach Antler Creek and farther."

"Cameronton?" I asked.

"The mule train won't, but you folks maybe could, if the rain holds off." We all looked at the sky, brilliant blue except for a few light clouds.

"Archie, Mr. McNaughton, can we?"

Archie didn't even glance at me, only at his wife. "You look tired, my dear," he said to her. "I long to bring you to your home, but maybe it's best not to push."

"I'm sure you know best, Mr. McNaughton," she said. She took his arm and smiled at him.

Where was her spirit? Ma would have said her piece, and it wouldn't be to go slow, or that Papa knew best. If Ma had been like that, Papa would have gone off with the Overlanders by himself, and the rest of the family would still be stuck in Fort Garry!

Mrs. Mac got what she deserved, too. The next day was sunny. We stopped late in the afternoon, though the sun was still high in the sky. I wanted to climb up the hill. Cataline thought I'd be able to see Richfield, the first of the three mining towns on Williams Creek, and maybe Barkerville, but Mrs. Mac told me to sit down like a lady and say the times tables to myself. "Patience is a virtue, Lisa," she said.

I obeyed and muttered the numbers up to three times twelve before I got too angry to concentrate.

Storm clouds gathered in the night; lightning blazed in jagged streaks on the mountaintops, and thunder rolled. How could I ever have mistaken dynamite blasts for thunder? The earth shook; my ears hurt with the noise. Then the rain began to beat on our tent; soon, water ran in sheets across the floor, soaking all our bedding. It did not clear in the morning but turned for a while to hail; icy hailstones spooked the animals and made the rest of us miserable, cold, and wet to our skins.

"We'll find shelter at Richfield," said Cataline, and we did, in a roadhouse. Archie ordered whiskey for all the men and tea for "the ladies." The landlord built up the fire, and we took turns steaming in front of it while our sodden clothes began to dry. The room was packed with miners. "You know these parts?" a burly fellow asked Cataline.

"Yep."

"Where's Discovery?"

"I'd guess the richest diggings are Billy Barker's in Barkerville and Cariboo Cameron's in Cameronton," said Cataline, "but I've been gone for five, six weeks. Anybody could've found something better while I've been away. Keep asking, and you'll find out."

The hail turned into rain, and we went on, walking now on a proper road. Richfield turned into Barkerville, and Barkerville became Cameronton without much space between any of the three. People everywhere, women as well as men, hurried to get out of the rain. Many greeted Cataline as they passed, though nobody stopped to talk.

"More houses every day," said Cataline. He was right; raw logs had been squared off and notched to fit at the corners in plenty of new buildings, some that didn't even have a roof on yet.

"Duncan told me the Royal Engineers are coming to survey the towns and mark out lots for building," I said, "but plenty of houses are built already. What about them?"

"They'll fit them in," said Cataline, "like they've done in other places. Don't you worry."

Sometimes I looked up at the buildings as we went past, but I kept drier if I held my hood over my head and looked down at the ground as I walked. Mrs. Mac rode Queenie; she rode sidesaddle, her back very straight, looking elegant in a long black cloak. If I had been riding, I would have galloped ahead, but she made Queenie walk beside Archie. I asked maybe three times if we were there yet, and Archie kept saying, "Soon, soon," and we kept not getting there.

I knew already that all the ground along the creek was staked and most claims had diggings, though plenty of miners hadn't found any gold.

Huge wooden troughs loomed above us. "What are they?" I asked.

"Flumes," said Archie. "They carry water to wash the gold, like we did with our pan in the river, only here we start with crushers to break up the ore and then we put it through big sluices. Even if there is not very much gold in the rocks, we grind up so much rock that we get quite a bit, if our claims are any good. You'll see."

"Where are your claims?" I asked. "Will we go there first, or to your house?"

"Lisa, stop bothering Mr. McNaughton." Mrs. Mac sounded really cross. *I'm going to be alone with her all day if I can't go mining,* I realized suddenly. *It will be horrible.*

CHAPTER N° 9

Our new house was like most of the roadhouses, only nicer; it had an attic and a stairway up to it. Downstairs was all one big room. There was a fireplace with a chimney made out of stones and a big iron pole to hang the soup pot over the fire.

There were two rooms in the attic: a big one for Archie and Mrs. Mac, and a little one for me, with a wooden bed, not painted, and a mattress filled with sweet-smelling fresh straw. I'd never slept all by myself. I felt homesick for Mary Jane and baby Rose in Kamloops, even if

Mary Jane sometimes kicked me and Rose woke up and cried.

"Do you like it, Lisa?" Archie pointed to a little table made from rough boards, bare and unpainted like the bed. "There's your washstand. One of the mules has been packing a pitcher and wash basin and—you know, the rest of it."

Archie was too polite to say right out that there was a chamber pot to go under the bed if I needed it at night. I felt like laughing at him. When you are on the trail, you get used to finding a rock or a tree to go behind when you need it. Pantaloons are terrible to pull down, though, when you are squatting on the ground. After a while, I took out some stitching in the crotch. That solved the problem. I'm sure Ma noticed when she did the washing, but she never said anything, and she never stitched my pantaloons up again.

If you had to wait for a privy to use on the trail, you'd be mighty uncomfortable, and that's a fact. The privy out back of our new house was made of rough lumber, like everything else. Maybe I'd get slivers when I sat down. Ouch! When things were unpacked, though, out came a wooden seat with a lid, finer than what we had in Fort Garry. I was pleased, and I'm sure Mrs. Mac was pleased as well.

It was still light when everything had been unloaded and piled on the dirt floor in the big downstairs room. "Goodbye, Lisa," said Cataline. "You've livened up this trip for me."

"When will you be back?" I asked him.

"I dunno," he replied. "A month or two, maybe. You'll be an old hand by then." He waved as he went out the door.

"I'd best be off as well," said Archie. "I'm sure you ladies have plenty to occupy yourselves."

"You're going out to your claim," I said.

"Of course," he said sharply. "I must see my partners and introduce the new crew. We haven't hit pay dirt, or I'd have heard, but I must inspect the work."

"Take me, please," I begged.

"No." He started to say more but caught his wife's eye, turned, and hurried out the door.

"Lisa," said Mrs. Mac, "can't you see that Mr. McNaughton has important matters to attend to? You must stop bothering him. Besides, he's right. You and I have work to do here."

So that was my first day in Cameronton, a mixture of good things and bad. The new bed smelled lovely, but I lay awake for a long time; Mrs. Mac would not have liked my thoughts.

CHAPTER N° 10

We were all up early the next morning.
I had filled my pitcher from the rain barrel, so I
had water for a wash in my new wash basin.
The china set was painted with pink rosebuds,
the prettiest I had ever seen.

"Did you pick it out?" I asked Archie. He
smiled at his wife.

"It came from Montreal," she said. "I used it
when I was your age, Lisa. I hoped you would
like it too."

"It is beautiful," I said. The knot in my stomach
eased.

It eased some more when Archie said we were all going out to the diggings after breakfast. "I want my ladies to see what we're doing," he said. "This could be our lucky day!"

He talked as we went, bending towards his wife's ear. I couldn't hear much. So much noise! The air rang: metal clanged against metal; wood thudded; water rushed; and everywhere, people shouted at each other. The road where we walked was full of people; the patches of ground between us and the creek were full of machinery and men, pulling on ropes, digging with spades, or hammering away at various wooden structures.

Interrupting a grown-up is rude, but soon I had to start asking questions. "Mr. McNaughton," I said, "what are those wheels doing?" I pointed to a huge wooden wheel, the third one we had passed. The wheel turned slowly as we watched. Like the others, this wheel had shelves sticking out from the rim, and water from them ran down into one of the long wooden flumes.

"That's a Cornish Wheel," said Archie. "Water gets into the mine, you see, and the wheel pumps it out so the diggers can work. We're going to set up a wheel like that at our diggings. I'll show you when we get there."

"This is a dangerous business," said Mrs. Mac slowly. "Are men hurt often, killed perhaps? I shall worry about you, my dear."

"The typhoid has killed more than the mines have," said Archie. "We are very careful. So far, all has been well with our crew. There are risks, of course, but there are also rewards. Think of the rewards, my love. There is a thrill in this business like no other. Every day, I go to work thinking, 'This may be the day we strike it lucky.'"

"Gold," I breathed. "Maybe today."

"There is a good chance of it." Archie's blue eyes gleamed. He was talking to me now; I was as excited as he was. "We are almost through the blue clay. That's where the gold is here, under the blue clay. Not everywhere, of course. It's not a sure thing, but our claims are in a line from Cariboo Cameron himself. They say his company has taken almost half a million dollars' worth of gold."

Half a million! Mountains of gold bars, hills of gold dust! How many wagons would we need to move half a million dollars' worth of gold to Victoria? I found out later that it was more like a quarter of a million dollars Cariboo Cameron had taken, but even so, that's a mighty fortune, even if his wife did die of the typhoid.

"Here we are," said Archie proudly. "Five men in our company, and we own seven claims, one hundred feet each, all licensed and recorded. There's the shaft."

We walked over. Three tall, straight trees had been notched and leaned together to make a tripod over a big hole in the ground. I could see timbers lining the hole, making a kind of collar. A rope with a big bucket on the end of it hung from the top of the tripod. "Lower away, boys," boomed a big man.

I knew that voice! "Mr. Wattie!" I exclaimed.

"Lisa! Good to see you, girlie." The big man smiled and bent to pat my shoulder. His long beard tickled my forehead.

"Mrs. McNaughton, this is my partner, James Wattie," said Archie. "I've told you about him, my dear. This is the man who taught Lisa and me how to pan for gold."

Of course, I wanted to go down in the shaft with Archie and Mr. Wattie. I wanted to see the blue clay. I wanted to dig the first shovelful that had gold nuggets.

"I want to go down." My words bursted out.

"Don't be ridiculous, Lisa," said Mrs. Mac.

I almost broke loose and ran to climb down the ladder that disappeared into the dark hole in the ground. Archie could see what I was thinking; he shook his head. He and Mr. Wattie started down, spades in hand.

I went over to the pile of dirt and stones that had once filled the space where there was now a hole, a shaft. I kicked the rocks, scuffing my boots. A pickaxe lay beside the pile. I hoisted it and swung down to split one rock, then another. The axe was heavy, but I was so angry I hardly noticed. I didn't even think about what Mrs. Mac would do. If she said anything, I didn't hear it.

The third rock split. As the two pieces fell, as I raised the axe again, something glittered. I held my breath. I got down on my knees in the dirt, not even thinking about my dress or my petticoat, and picked up the piece of rock. If there was gold in it, it wasn't ordinary rock. It was ore, the stuff you mine. And this was a nugget of gold, no doubt of it. The soft, rich, buttery sheen could not be mistaken.

"Gold!" I screamed at Mrs. Mac. Then I ran over to the shaft. "Archie," I yelled into the echoing darkness, "Mr. Wattie, Discovery's *here*. I've found Cariboo gold!"

*The axe was heavy, but I was
so angry I hardly noticed.
I didn't even think about
what Mrs. Mac would do.*

ACKNOWLEDGMENTS

As with Book One, *Overland to Cariboo,* many people have helped with my research. Elizabeth Duckworth of the Kamloops Museum sent me a magnificent bundle of newspaper articles and unpublished records about the area and the Schubert family. Marg Brimacombe of Kamloops provided contact names and descriptions. Mickey King, archivist with the Sisters of Saint Ann, generously emailed much information about the Oblate Missionaries of the period, as well as about the sister Order of St. Ann. The Internet yielded many treasures, most notably from Isobel Bescoby's unpublished M.A. thesis (University of British Columbia, 1932, *Some Aspects of Society in Cariboo from Its Discovery until 1871*). Quotations and references to this study turned up in many other works (e.g., *Miners at Work: A History of British Columbia's Gold Rushes,* by B. Griffin, Royal British Columbia Museum, Victoria, B.C., consulted at http://www.em.gov.bc.ca/Mining/Geolsurv/Publications/OpenFiles/OF1992-16-Pioneer/GoldRush.html). Isobel Bescoby was my teacher for two years at the Model School in Victoria in the 1930s and a family friend later in Ottawa. Little did I think I would owe her a debt of gratitude for her research as well as for her teaching! W. Champness's record, *To Cariboo and Back in 1862,* was published in 1972; a reprint appears on the Barkerville webpage, http://www.barkerville.ca. Cemetery records, histories of hostelries, maps, and details of the construction of the wagon road, a marvel of road-building over hostile terrain, were all found on the Internet.

Library research, particularly at the University of Toronto's Robarts Library, led to helpful publications by authors such as Marian Place, Branwen C. Patenaude, Fred Ludditt, Noel G. Duclos, and Richard Thomas Wright. My writing group has provided support and criticism for more than twenty years; thanks, Ayanna, Barb, Heather, Lorraine, Sylvia, and Vancy.

Dear Reader,

Welcome back to the continuing adventures of Our Canadian Girl! It's been another exciting year for us here at Penguin, publishing new stories and continuing the adventures of twelve terrific girls. The best part of this past year, though, has been the wonderful letters we've received from readers like you, telling us about your favourite Our Canadian Girl story, and the parts you liked the most. Best of all, you told us which stories you would like to read, and we were amazed! There are so many remarkable stories in Canadian history. It seems that wherever we live, great stories live too, in our towns and cities, on our rivers and mountains. Thank you so much for sharing them.

So please, stay in touch. Write letters, log on to our website (www.ourcanadiangirl.ca), let us know what you think of Our Canadian Girl. We're listening.

Sincerely,
    Barbara Berson

Canada's

1608
Samuel de
Champlain
establishes
the first
fortified
trading post
at Quebec.

1759
The British
defeat the
French in
the Battle
of the
Plains of
Abraham.

1812
The United
States
declares war
against
Canada.

1845
The expedition of
Sir John Franklin
to the Arctic ends
when the ship is
frozen in the pack
ice; the fate of its
crew remains a
mystery.

1869
Louis Riel
leads his
Metis
followers in
the Red
River
Rebellion.

1871
British
Columbia
joins
Canada.

1755
The British
expel the
entire French
population
of Acadia
(today's
Maritime
provinces),
sending
them into
exile.

1776
The 13
Colonies
revolt
against
Britain, and
the Loyalists
flee to
Canada.

1837
Calling for
responsible
government, the
Patriotes, following
Louis-Joseph
Papineau, rebel in
Lower Canada;
William Lyon
Mackenzie leads the
uprising in Upper
Canada.

1867
New
Brunswick,
Nova Scotia,
and the United
Province of
Canada come
together in
Confederation
to form the
Dominion of
Canada.

1870
Manitoba joins
Canada. The
Northwest
Territories
become an
official
territory of
Canada.

1762
Elizabeth

1862
Lisa

Timeline

1885
At Craigellachie, British Columbia, the last spike is driven to complete the building of the Canadian Pacific Railway.

1898
The Yukon Territory becomes an official territory of Canada.

1914
Britain declares war on Germany, and Canada, because of its ties to Britain, is at war too.

1918
As a result of the Wartime Elections Act, the women of Canada are given the right to vote in federal elections.

1945
World War II ends conclusively with the dropping of atomic bombs on Hiroshima and Nagasaki.

1873
Prince Edward Island joins Canada.

1896
Gold is discovered on Bonanza Creek, a tributary of the Klondike River.

1905
Alberta and Saskatchewan join Canada.

1917
In the Halifax harbour, two ships collide, causing an explosion that leaves more than 1,600 dead and 9,000 injured.

1939
Canada declares war on Germany seven days after war is declared by Britain and France.

1949
Newfoundland, under the leadership of Joey Smallwood, joins Canada.

1897
Emily

1939
Ellen

Read more about Lisa
in Book One
Overland to Cariboo

It's 1861, and Lisa and her family cross prairies, scale mountains, and ford dangerous rivers on their journey to the goldfields of British Columbia.

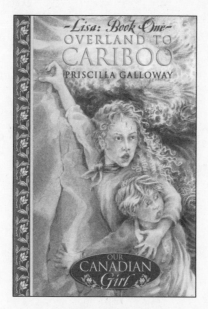

Lisa's third book is due to be published in spring 2006!